There was a surprised hush. Yasmin forced herself to speak.

"I have four kittens. I must find them homes by Saturday. If I don't, I have to take them to the Cats' Protection. I'll never know what has happened to them. Please, please, will you help me? I know that you can't take them yourselves but perhaps your mother or neighbour may know someone who wants a kitten. Will you ask? Just ask? Thank you."

She stumbled back to her seat. Ella leaned over to pat her shoulder. "There! That wasn't so bad, was it?"

Young Corgi books are perfect when you are looking for great books to read on your own. They are full of exciting stories and entertaining pictures. There are funny books, scary books, spine-tingling stories and mysterious ones. Whatever your interests you'll find something in Young Corgi to suit you: from families to football, from animals to ghosts. The books are written by some of the most famous and popular of today's children's authors, and by some of the best new talents, too.

Whether you read one chapter a night, or devour the whole book in one sitting, you'll love Young Corgi Books. The more you read, the more you'll want to read!

Other Young Corgi Books to get your teeth into:
SINK OR SWIM by Ghillian Potts
A WITCH IN THE CLASSROOM! by Ghillian Potts
PATRICK THE PARTY-HATER by Emily Smith
BILLY AND THE SEAGULLS by Paul May

DIARY DAYS

Ghillian Potts

Illustrated by Leighton Noyes

YOUNG CORGI

DIARY DAYS
A YOUNG CORGI BOOK : 0 552 54686 0

Published in Great Britain by Young Corgi,
an imprint of Random House Children's Books

This edition published 2005

1 3 5 7 9 10 8 6 4 2

Papers used by Random House Children's Books are natural, recyclable
products made from wood grown in sustainable forests. The manufacturing
processes conform to the environmental regulations of the country of origin.

Set in 16/20pt Bembo Schoolbook

Young Corgi Books are published by Random House Children's Books
61–63 Uxbridge Road, London W5 5SA,
a division of The Random House Group Ltd,
in Australia by Random House Australia (Pty) Ltd,
20 Alfred Street, Milsons Point, Sydney, NSW 2061, Australia,
in New Zealand by Random House New Zealand Ltd,
18 Poland Road, Glenfield, Auckland 10, New Zealand
and in South Africa by Random House (Pty) Ltd,
Endulini, 5a Jubilee Road, Parktown 2193, South Africa

THE RANDOM HOUSE GROUP Limited Reg. No. 954009

www.kidsatrandomhouse.co.uk

A CIP catalogue record for this book is available from the British Library.

Printed and bound in Great Britain by
Cox & Wyman Ltd, Reading, Berkshire.

To the children of Gordon School, Eltham,
for their help and advice; and to my
granddaughter Hazel, for hers.
And to all the people who love
and protect helpless animals.

Chapter One: Monday

Kitten Countdown: 6

It was nearly going-home time. Mr
Williams had collected a pile of notebooks. He put them tidily on the table
and smiled at his class.

Yasmin wondered what he was so
happy about. It usually meant he had
some new idea, one that the class
probably wouldn't enjoy.

She tried to listen to Mr Williams.
No. It was no good. She could think of
nothing but Lady, her little cat, and

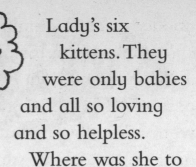

Lady's six kittens. They were only babies and all so loving and so helpless.

Where was she to find homes for six kittens? In a week? But she must. Somehow. *I must, must find them homes!*

"What have we been studying lately?" Mr Williams's smile faded as he gazed at the blank faces in front of him. "Can anyone tell me? Scott? Ella? Yasmin? Mike?"

Yasmin tried to gather her scattered thoughts. What was he talking about?

Slowly Ella put up her hand. Mr Williams

nodded encouragingly. "Yes, Ella?"

"People. In History. Keeping diaries."

"Yes! Thank you, Ella. People in the past who kept diaries. Ordinary people who wrote down what happened to them, every day, or sometimes just when something exciting happened. Such diaries are very useful to historians. Why is that, Connor?"

Connor sank down in his chair but he couldn't vanish. "Tells them ordinary things," he mumbled.

"Right! Ordinary things! Like what they had for breakfast or what they saw at the theatre. How much they paid for their clothes. All sorts of useful ordinary information. Now, I want all of you to keep a diary for one week, starting tonight. Record what you do each day – What is it, Mike?"

"I'm not doing schoolwork on a Saturday!"

"Saturday is a day, just like today. It won't hurt you to note down where you go and anything interesting you see," said Mr Williams firmly.

"I'm going shopping with my nan, Saturday," announced Ella. "We're going up the market—"

"Thank you, Ella. You can write it all down in your diary." Mr Williams picked up the pile of small notebooks. "Oh, Yasmin. Would you hand these out? Thank you."

Yasmin squeezed out of her seat and began giving out the little green notebooks. Her face felt hot. She kept her head down and didn't look at anyone except her friend Ella. Ella would have liked to hand out the books. I wish Mr Williams had asked Ella, she thought. Or anyone. Anyone but me!

Mr Williams went on talking. "You can write your diaries in these books.

You'll see the first page already has today, Monday, written at the top. Put your name on the cover now. Next Monday I shall collect them and  we'll see what you have recorded for the historians of the future! In a hundred years from now, they will be delighted to find your accounts of your week."

"We won't be here in a hundred years!" Connor protested.

"Oh, you might be. But you'd probably be too old to remember what you did when you were ten."

"Do *you* remember what you did when you were ten, Mr Williams?" asked Katie.

Mr Williams didn't answer.

"Hey, Scott! I'm going to pretend to be a detective. That'd be interesting!" announced Nick.

"Yes! Great idea, Nick. Let's all pretend to be someone interesting," Scott agreed at the top of his voice.

Yasmin couldn't help giggling. It was so like Scott to want to be interesting. And noisy.

"*QUIET!!*"

Silence.

"Has everyone got a diary? Good. You have seven days. Start tonight. I don't expect you to write very much each day, but I do expect you to think about what you write. OK, off you go. See you tomorrow."

Yasmin's Diary
MONDAY.

I do not think I want someone a hundred years from now to read my thoughts. So when Mr Williams gives us back our work I shall tear this up and burn it. Ella likes everyone to know what she does but I do not. We are friends but we are so different. Today I told Ella and Alice and several other people about the kittens but no one wants one. They say their mum won't let them have one. Or they have a dog or a cat already. It is not easy to ask. People don't want to listen.

She
stopped for a
moment and
thought of the
kittens.

Meep

Boots

She thought
of Meep, and his
happy pounces on
his mother's tail.

Then Mittens, with her smart black
and brown stripes and dainty white paws.

And Moppet clambering over the
other kittens only to fall off, surprised
and waving her paws in the air.

She thought of Boots, his black
fur and his white fluffy hind
legs making him look like
Puss in Boots.

Mittens

Moppet

And Patch, the opposite of Boots, almost all white with her lop-sided patch of black over one eye.

Patch

Oh, and Thingamubob! The smallest and weakest, so tiny in her striped coat of grey and darker grey.

Thingamubob

She started to write again.

Ella said "Why not ask the teachers?" But I can't. I am scared to. Ella does not understand why I am so worried about the kittens but she will try to help me find homes for them. She is a very good friend and a kind person. I did not ask the boys. Some of them heard what I said, but I did not ask. Boys don't care. Scott was horrid. He said I was stupid. Nick did, too.

She couldn't bear to remember what else they had said. It made her feel sick. But it kept going round and round in her head.

No! she thought. No! I won't believe it! Scott just said it to frighten me. But suppose it's true?

She couldn't write that down. It would make it too real.

Yasmin sighed and slipped the little notebook into her schoolbag. Then she took it out again. She didn't want anyone to see it before she handed it in. Where could she hide it?

The big chest of drawers! It reached almost to the floor on its old-fashioned flat round feet. Yasmin poked the notebook carefully into the small gap underneath it. She stood back to check that it was invisible. Then she went downstairs to help her mother get supper.

Her cat, Lady, came purring from her basket, followed by her family. All six of them. Yasmin hastily tried to stuff them back but Mum had seen them.

"Yasmin. Those kittens must go by Saturday."

"You said a week!" Yasmin wailed. "I thought . . ."

"I am sorry, pet. I meant this week. Oh, my dear, I know you wish to keep them and for them to be happy. I wish it, too, but we cannot keep them. It is impossible. We must take them to the Cat Protection people. They will try to find them homes, I'm sure they will."

"But I'll never know what's happened to them!" Yasmin burst out. She knew she couldn't keep them. Even though they were still little, the food for the kittens cost too much and kittens grow! Seven cats would be far too many for their small house. Her hand tightened on Meep, her favourite. The warm soft body trembled with his baby purr. Her eyes prickled with tears. She blinked hard and tried to keep her voice steady.

"Mum, I'll go and put a notice in the papershop window this evening. May I have a postcard and write it now?"

Yasmin made the card look as interesting as possible, with different coloured pens and her most careful printing. She drew a cat face on it.

HEALTHY KITTENS NEED GOOD HOMES she wrote. MALE AND FEMALE. BLACK AND WHITE OR SILVER TABBY. She put her phone number and address at the bottom.

Then she took it along to the newsagents.

Mrs Fenton smiled at her. She knew Yasmin because she often came to the little shop when Mum had run out of milk or bread. Yasmin wasn't shy with her. She smiled back.

Mrs Fenton looked at the card. "Kittens, is it? Well, my dear, I was thinking I should have another cat. But it must be a tom. I can't be doing with a female."

Yasmin gazed at her. "Oh! Mrs Fenton, you are a miracle! I will go at once and fetch the two toms, so you can choose. Thank you! Oh, thank you!"

She ran home as fast as she could. At least one kitten was saved. I hope she chooses Meep, she thought. Who could resist him?

That evening she added to her diary.

I have a home for Meep! I shall miss him. But I hope he will be happy. Now there are five left. If only they were all toms! People don't want girl cats, because of having kittens.

Nick's Diary
MONDAY.
This diary rubbish is going to be a bore, I reckon. Still, me and

Scott mean to have a bit of
fun with it. He's going to be a
detective with me. He thinks I
don't know he's being Spiderman
as well, but everyone knows that
Scott had a really wicked
Spiderman outfit last birthday.
So I'm going to be a detective.
And an SAS man.
If Scott thinks
he can tell me
what to do,
I'll tell him
the SAS can
tell the police
to go jump in
the lake.
I got the
beret and the
flak jacket
anyway. Paid
for them

myself in the surplus shop.
Scott's not going to shoot me
with a grotty Spiderman web
blaster!
That Yasmin was going round
whining about her kittens today.
Scott told her if you give them
to the Cat Protection, the
kittens get killed after a week,
like at Battersea Dogs Home.
Ha ha. I don't think it's true,
but of course she believed it.
She didn't half look sick. Girls
are soft. They'd be no good at
SAS and fighting.

Scott's Diary
MONDAY.

This is the log book of Detective
Constable Scott Bailey.
Although DC Nick Smith does not
suspect a thing, I am really

Spiderman and I could transform myself and swoop onto the criminals but I can't without him knowing. What we ought to do is, we ought to follow suspicious people and catch them burgling. That'd be wicked, that would . . .

Ella's Diary
MONDAY.

I mean to make this really interesting. Lots of things can happen in a week, after all. It'd be easier if it didn't have to be true. Then I could save someone from a fire and tell how brave I was. But I shan't. Perhaps I can make something happen . . .

I just now heard a car's brakes screaming so I went to look. Nothing to see. But it reminded me about when Mrs Howard next door's cat got run over. It was a really stupid lazy cat and it used to lie in the road. That's how it got run over. The lady what did it was ever so upset. She cried and everything.

That was weeks ago but I heard Mrs Howard only yesterday telling Mum she still misses it. Hey! Maybe she'd take one of Yas's kittens! I must tell Yas tomorrow. She'll be pleased! She does worry about them kittens. Ever since she found the mother cat all thin and scared. 'Course she didn't know it was going to have kittens and her mum wasn't best pleased, was she, because they do cost money for food and that, and I don't think Yas

and her mum have much money.
The cat's called Lady. I helped
name the kittens. They're ace.

Alice's Diary
MONDAY. First day of Diary
FOOD (like Mr Williams said).
For breakfast today I had a
boiled egg and Mum and
Dad had bacon and
Megan had baby gunk,
same as she always
does. Some of it has
fruit in it and some has
cheese or whatever. For supper
tonight we had tomato soup and
fish pie and trifle. Megan had
some of the soup and
a bit of fish and
trifle. She
banged her
spoon on the

table so hard that a lump of trifle came off and went splat on Dermot. He's our huge great soppy Irish wolfhound. He didn't mind. Just licked it off. Mum says he'll want trifle now as well as all the other things he eats. Which is anything he can get hold of.

Mike's Diary
MONDAY.
Given notebooks for diary. Stupid.
  My brother Jack went out. To see some girl, I suppose.
  Dad's on nights this week. Wish he wasn't.

Chapter Two: Tuesday

Kitten Countdown: 5

Yasmin looked round the playground for Ella. She's going to be late again, she worried. She joined the line at the door, still peering over her shoulder.

The school door opened and everyone began to squeeze in.

Feet pounded behind her.

"Yas!" Ella rushed up, out of breath.

Yasmin jumped. "What is it? What's wrong?"

"Nothing. Listen, you remember the

cat next door to me that got run over? Mrs Howard's cat?"

"Oh yes, of course, I remember, poor thing! But what . . ."

"No, but listen, Yas! I see Mrs Howard this morning when she's putting out the rubbish. I go, 'Do you want a kitten because my friend Yasmin has a cat with kittens that she has to get rid of soon,' but she sniffs a lot and goes, 'Not now, dear,' and then she went indoors to make a cup of tea. But she never said, 'No'. I think she will want one . . ."

Yasmin smiled at Ella. "You are such a good friend, Ella! I – I will go to her. Soon." If I am brave enough, she thought, miserably.

Mr Williams picked up the register. "All right, settle down, everyone." He called the register, much faster than usual. Mike came in late, scowling.

Mr Williams sighed and waited until Mike had stomped to his table. "This afternoon, as you know, we have Art." He smiled at them. "Now, do you remember that there is a competition for the best flower paintings?"

Several people muttered "Yes". Several other people said "No!" quite loudly. Mr Williams went on as if he hadn't heard.

"Now, it's not just the best in this school but in all the schools in the borough. Today, we are going to paint flowers. Each of you will have a flower, not all the same flowers, and each of you will do his or her best."

Yasmin stared at her hands. She didn't like Art. She knew she would get a flower that she couldn't paint. She would be a failure. She felt so miserable that she almost missed Ella's whisper.

"Look at Mike!"

Yasmin looked. Mike was pale. There were dark patches under his eyes. Whatever was wrong with him? Was he ill?

But at that moment Mr Williams told them to line up for Assembly and she saw Mike get up with everyone else. So he couldn't be too ill.

All the same, she kept away from him. I mustn't catch whatever he's got, she told herself. I can't be ill. I've got to find homes for the kittens.

The row in the Art class that afternoon was the worst ever. Mike yelled at Mr Williams and screwed up his painting and flung it across the room. Then he dragged his chair over to the window and sat with his back to the room, silent.

Yasmin and Ella were not the only ones to crouch in their chairs, shaking. Even Alice looked worried.

"Mike *must* be ill," Yasmin whispered to Ella.

Ella bit her lip. "I think he thinks that his dad doesn't like him," she murmured.

"Not like him?" Yasmin was shocked. "But dads are supposed to love you! They are, aren't they?" she added doubtfully.

"My dad loves me," said Ella. "See, Mike's mum died. His dad has to work shifts. He leaves Mike and his big brother Jack to look after themselves, my nan says."

"Oh." said Yasmin. "My father didn't have a job when he went away."

She wondered if having a job meant your father loved you. Did not having one make him stop loving you?

Mr Williams picked up Mike's painting, smoothed it out and looked at it sadly. Then he went on as if nothing had happened.

Yasmin sneaked a look at the painting at the end of school. It was not a painting of a flower. It was a black motorbike with a pool of red beside it. Like blood. She shuddered. Why did Mike always paint motorbikes?

It was as if he wanted to be like a machine . . . Machines don't cry. But they don't bleed, either.

Yasmin's Diary

Tuesday

Today we had to do flower paintings. The best pictures will go to a competition. Then the winners will paint a mural. My paintings are always too small. Mr Williams says "Fill the paper! Big strokes!" but I can't do that. I am a person who paints small things. I do not paint big splashy things. So I am no use for a mural. I think the teachers should understand that not all people can do the same things. Mr Williams did not try to make Mike paint flowers, big or little. Why not?

If I were to scream and hit people, would I be left to paint small? Should I perhaps try it, Mr Williams? On Thursday, when we have to paint again! Or shall I paint my kittens? Perhaps I will. Yes, I shall paint Meep now, at once, so I will always remember just how he looked.

There!

After Tea

The kind papershop lady has just telephoned. Her sister wants a kitten! A female! I am so happy. I shall give her Moppet.

This is
Moppet.

I did ask the
teachers today –
well, I asked Miss
Chell and Mrs Arksy
at playtime but I
can't make myself go to
the Staff Room and ask
them all. I tried but I could
not knock. It is shaming to
be so afraid.

Yasmin put her diary away again.
Her throat felt tight with misery. She bit
her fingers. "I am a coward," she
whispered.

She went to find a basket for
Moppet. "I *must* learn to be brave, for
the kittens," she told herself. "Tomorrow
I will tell *everybody* about them. I will
ask and ask and beg them to help.

Perhaps the people in my class would look for homes for Mittens and Boots and Patch and Thingamubob. Maybe? If I asked the whole class?"

But the thought of standing up in front of everyone made her stomach feel cold. "I can't!" she said aloud. "I *can't*! But I must." She hugged her stomach and tried to stop shivering.

Alice's Diary

Tues.

Mike was late today. He was cross all yesterday and he's still cross today. He can paint really well but he only does motorbikes. I don't know why. I did ask him one time but he just walked off. My mum says to leave him be, because he hasn't got over his mum dying.

I painted the flower Mr Williams

said to paint, but it wasn't no
good. It was awful. I bet
when we all have to paint
some more, Thursday,
mine will be rotten. Again.

Dad's got some new
stinky cheese. Italian. I didn't
give Megan any. Mum said not to,
in case she can't dijest it. (She's
only just one year old. Birthday
party last week.)

We had a stew with peppers in,
the big ones not the hot ones. I
don't like the hot ones. Mum says
she doesn't either but Dad does.
He cooks sometimes and once I
couldn't eat it at all because of all
the spices. And
we had fruit
after, and the
stinky cheese.

Mike's Diary

Tues.
Got to school late.
Given extra work.
Forgot dinner money. I
hate painting. Dad at
home with bad head.

Chapter Three: Wednesday

Kitten Countdown: 4

Yasmin gulped as if she could swallow down her fear, like medicine. Mr Williams had said she might speak to the whole class before they went to Assembly but now her mouth was so dry that she could barely whisper. She stood in front of the class and shivered.

"Come along, Yasmin!" Mr Williams was trying to be kind but he was in a hurry, as usual.

"Please . . ." began Yasmin. Her voice

was lost in the buzz of talk. She felt her eyes prickle. No! I must not cry! she told herself.

Ella suddenly jumped up. "Shut up, the lot of you!" she yelled. "Yasmin's got something to say!"

There was a surprised hush. Yasmin forced herself to speak.

"I have four kittens. I must find them homes by Saturday. If I don't, I have to take them to the Cats' Protection. I'll never know what has happened to them. Please, please, will you help me? I know that you can't take them yourselves but perhaps your mother or neighbour may know someone who wants a kitten. Will you ask? Just ask? Thank you."

She stumbled back to her seat. Ella leaned over to pat her shoulder. "There! That wasn't so bad, was it? I'll ask my nan, soon as I see her.

My nan knows everyone. She'll help!"

Yasmin blew her nose, trying to hide tears of relief. No one had said anything horrible. Lots of people were talking about kittens. She smiled at Ella.

"Line up for Assembly," called Mr Williams. "Quiet now." He nodded to Yasmin as she passed. "Well done."

Yasmin went red. She wanted to say something but she couldn't think of anything sensible. She was saved by Mike barging into the classroom, later than ever. Mr Williams at once turned his frown on Mike. Yasmin slipped away.

Yasmin's Diary

Wednesday

It was very hard to speak to all the class. I could not have done it for myself - but for the kittens, I did.

Lots of people have said they will help. Connor has promised to ask his aunty if his cousin can have a kitten and Katie says she knows a nice old man who loves cats. And there is Ella's Nan. I think she will be the most helpful. Only, how <u>soon</u> can

they do anything? There is so
little time left. I <u>wish</u> I had
asked sooner. No one has even
looked at my card in the
newsagent's since I put it
there. I went down this evening
and asked. No one.

I saw Scott and Nick on the
way back. They acted so
strangely, as if they did not
want to be seen. Nick said on
Monday that he would pretend to
be a detective. He meant, in
his diary, not really and truly.
He is silly, especially when he
is with Scott. Scott pretends
all sorts of things. I think he
doesn't know when he is telling
lies. Are they detecting for
real, now? But what would they
detect? Me?

I told Mum about speaking to

the class, and she said she was proud of me!

Nick's Diary
Wednesday
Me and Scott think we should just be detectives. He did want to be Spiderman but he says you can't be Spiderman at school. It's all very well in America, they have all these lockers and you can hide your Spiderman outfit but we only have pegs in the cloak- room, so what's the use? And they took

away the proper telephone boxes and now they're all open. You can't change into Spiderman in the middle of the path! So this evening we went out after tea to find good houses to burgle. Then we can stake them out in case somebody comes along to burgle them. And then we detect them.

Saw Yasmin. She didn't see us, as we were lurking. She was making a right fuss this morning about her kittens.

Went past Mike's house and heard someone shouting. That's nothing new. His dad shouts a lot.

We didn't find anyone to detect, so we went home.

Alice's Diary

Wed. (in case you hadn't guessed)
That Yasmin really really surprised
me. She stood up in front of the
whole class (all except Mike, he
was late of course) and asked us
to find homes for her kittens. I
always thought she was a total
wimp. So maybe she will find them
homes.

Mike got sent to the Head
because he was late again today.
He was sat in the corridor to
write something. He wouldn't say
what. I wonder what Mrs Kaye
does make people write when they
keep being late. I never was late
more than once at a time so I
don't know. Scott was being really
silly about what he's doing for his
diary. I think he's being
Spiderman. He got a Spiderman

outfit for his birthday. It's OK writing this because by the time Mr Williams sees my diary, he'll have seen Scott's too. I'm getting quite sorry for him (Mr Williams, I mean). He'll have an awful lot of really boring stuff to read.

For tea we had scrambled eggs. With anchovies in.

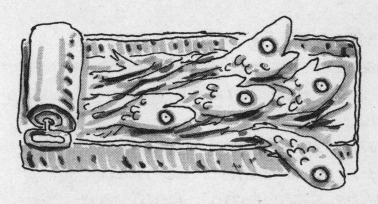

Ella's Diary

Wednesday. I just couldn't believe it when Yas got up and talked to the class today. Yas! She can't say boo to a goose, my nan says. My

nan is going to see if one of her
mates can take a kitten. She says
she likes to stick her nose in other
people's business. But she only
does it to help. Mum says I'm like
Nan. Dad says so too. I'm glad. I
like my nan. (She's Dad's mum, not
Mum's.) I like my granma and
granpa too, of course.

Mike's Diary

Wed
Got to school really
late sent to the Head.
My brother Jack's girl-
friend come to tea.
She's boring. Dad out
to work after. I wish
~~he'd talk to me sometimes~~

Chapter Four: Thursday

Kitten Countdown: 4

In the morning, Yasmin felt happier at first. Almost everyone in her class had asked somebody about the kittens. Connor had asked an aunt. Ella had gone round to her nan and her nan meant to ask around that very day.

"I'll tell you what she says this evening," promised Ella.

Alice had actually gone into the supermarket and told the manager that they should have a cat! He'd said they weren't allowed to because they sold food. Yasmin was breathless with admiration just the same.

"How brave you are, Alice!" she said.

Alice shrugged. "Didn't work."

"Great try, though," said Connor.

People in other classes had heard about the kittens. They came over at playtime and told Yasmin how they'd like to help but . . . Yasmin smiled and smiled and said, "Thank you. You are so kind!" over and over. She felt as if her face was on fire but she went on smiling.

The Head stopped Yasmin on the stairs and said she wished she could help. "But my husband is allergic to cat hair," she explained. "Cats make him sneeze and sneeze and come out in a nasty rash. I'm so sorry, Yasmin."

Yasmin's cheeks ached with smiling. It was almost a relief to start painting.

Nobody bothered her then. Except Mike.

He'd cut his hand in the playground at dinner time. He charged round smearing blood from it on people's work. Yasmin didn't even try to stop him spoiling her painting. He looked more miserable than she could bear.

Alice shrieked and swiped at him, Nick yelled for Mr Williams to stop him and Ella whisked her painting away before he could reach her. She scrambled up onto her chair and held it out of his reach.

Mr Williams took him to the Head and came back frowning.

Yasmin turned the smear of blood into a leaf. It had dried to a dull reddish brown and did look like a dead leaf.

Connor looked over her shoulder. "If you look at blood through a microscope," he said, "it's just yellow. Not red at all. Funny, isn't it?"

Yasmin nodded and went on painting. Her hand shook and she wanted to cry. No one had found a home for the kittens. It was all her fault. If she'd only been brave sooner! It was almost too late now. Only this evening and tomorrow and then . . .

Perhaps Ella's nan would find someone? She might have found someone already and be waiting to tell Ella. And then Ella would come rushing round to tell her.

She tried hard to believe it.

Yasmin's Diary

Thursday evening

Ella hasn't come round. So her Nan cannot find a home for any of the kittens. I still have to find homes for the four of them. Tomorrow! Can I go to the poor lady whose cat was run over? Perhaps I may go tomorrow. Ella says that the old cat was striped. Suppose I take Patch and Boots with me. They are both black and white, without any stripes at all.

At school today Mike had a fight. I don't know what about. I do not want to see fights.

10pm: Ella rang up! Her Nan has found a home for one of the kittens! We are to take the

kitten to Nan's house tomorrow
before school. Ella says there is
a little boy who wants a kitten
very much and his mother says
they will have a female because
they are more loving! I shall
take Mittens.
Thingamubob is
too little for a
child to
play with.
   This is
what Mittens
looks like.
   That is half of them saved.

Scott's Diary

Thursday
It's getting really stupid, trying
to be detectives. I told Nick I've
had enough. We haven't spotted
one single thing, all the time we've

been watching. So let him go off
and be a SAS on his own. See if I
care. I reckon Spiderman can do
without a sidekick.

Only I can't be Spiderman in
school. And it's not all that easy
getting out after tea, either.
Tonight I found a lost dog. Well,
I think it was lost. It acted
lost. I took it to its home. The
people weren't very pleased.

I wish I had a dog. I'd like a
collie. Or a husky. Not one of the
silly little yapping ones, like my
auntie has. It bit me one time. My
ankle bled like anything. Well, quite
a lot. Mum put this really burning
stuff on. She says dog bites can
be dangerous. No one put anything
on Mike's hand today when it bled.
But it wasn't a dog bite.

Mike's Diary

Thurs.
Fell over in playground.
Nick tripped me. My
hand bled so I wiped it
on the paintings. Sent
to Head.
   Jack's girl round
again. Makes out she
likes me. Well, I
don't like her.
She's called
Sylvie. Soppy
name.
   Dad on late
shift still.
Never see him
these days.
Not properly.
   Wish I was
big as Jack.

Chapter Five: Friday

Kitten Countdown: 3

People were already forgetting about the kittens. One or two of the girls came to say sorry they couldn't help. Yasmin knew she was on her own again.

Ella was full of the visit to the market on Saturday. "You must come, Yas! Nan asked for you to come, didn't she? She wants you!"

Yasmin liked Ella's nan, specially since she'd found a home for Mittens.

"Yes, I'll come. Please thank your nan for asking me. But I have to help my mother on Saturdays. I can't stay long."

"You'll have fun. We always do," promised Ella.

Alice wanted to talk about what other people had put in their diaries. "Know what? Mr Williams said to say what we eat, so that's what I done! All of it."

"Nothing else? Just food? He'll get indigestion, reading it," giggled Patrick. "I've put in about footy, mostly."

"Wonder what Mike's written," said Nick.

"Nothing, most like." Alice shrugged. "Have you pretended to be a detective, like you said, Nick?"

Nick scraped his foot along the ground. "It got boring. So I thought, let's bore old Williams. So last night I wrote down my mum's shopping list and all the prices she paid, off the till whatsit. She does all the shopping of a Thursday, see."

They all laughed. "He can't say he didn't ask for it!" said Ella. "That's clever, Nick."

Yasmin tried to ignore the hollow feeling inside her. She talked as much as usual. She did her work. She ran after balls in the Games lesson. She smiled and pretended to be happy. But all the time there was the grey feeling of defeat.

Half saved is better than none, she told herself. Herself did not believe it.

She walked home with Ella.

"I wish I wasn't so scared of everything," she said out loud.

"Whatever do you mean? You're not! You're as brave as anybody," Ella protested. "What's the matter, Yas?"

"I think I must go to see your neighbour."

"Mrs Howard? She's nice, no need to worry. Hey, I'll come with you!"

Yasmin shook her head. "I must do this by myself. If she sends me away . . ." She stopped. If Mrs Howard sent her away, what could she do?

Ella stood still and peered at Yasmin. "You sure? I don't mind. I'll come if you want."

Yasmin was sure. "I'll go now. Now, this minute! Soon as I can fetch the kittens."

Alice's Diary

Friday

Cereal for breakfast. It's a new sort, full of nuts and stuff. Chewy. It's supposed to have heaps of minerals and vitamins in but Dad says it's mostly sugar and we shouldn't eat it. He never eats cereal. He says he gets enough minerals and vitamins anyway. My baby sister threw some on the floor. I cleared it up. She's so messy. Megan the Mess. Only then she held her arms out to me and said Ah-a. That's her way of saying Alice.

We had a new sort of cheese for tea but I can't spell the name. It was smelly but tasted OK. Megan wanted some so I gave her a tiny bit but she spat it out. She is yukky. Like that Mike, messing up our paintings yesterday. Boys are idiots, always fighting.

'Course, some girls are idiots, too. Like Yas and her precious kittens. I told her to have the mother cat operated on or there'll be another lot of kittens in no time! She went dead pale. I thought she was going to snivel but she just said, "Thank you, Alice". She's so polite! Softie.

Yasmin's Diary

Friday

I put Patch and Boots in the cat basket and took them round to Ella's neighbour, Mrs Howard, after school. She was very nice. I said I was sorry to come so soon after her cat's death but the kittens would be put down if I cannot find them homes. I said 'put down', not 'killed' because old ladies don't like

such words. I did not say it is
their last day. She cried a
little and I pretended not to
notice. Then she stroked them
and Boots climbed up on her and
Patch purred very loudly and –
she took them both! I was so
happy that I cried a little,
too. She says I must come
again and see how they are
getting on. It is like a reward
for being brave!
    This is Boots.

This is Patch.
Alice told
me something
today. I think
she <u>meant</u> to
be kind.

Yasmin stopped writing. "I must ask Mum," she decided. "Perhaps Alice is right but . . ."

She ran downstairs.

Her mum understood at once. "Yes, pet, I know. Lady can't keep on having kittens. If she has an operation, she won't get worn out with babies and she really won't miss them. Lots of cats have it. It's perfectly safe. We'll take her to the PDSA as soon as all the kittens are gone. She'll be all right, I promise."

Yasmin cuddled Lady until she mewed to go out.

Mike's Diary

Fri.

Hand still hurts. Lot of idiots saying me and Nick had a fight yesterday. We never. Nick come up right behind me and I turned round too fast and he fell down and tripped me so I fell over too. That's all.

   Dad at work again tonight. Jack's old enough to leave home. Why dont he? I mean to, soon as I can. Dad wont care.

Chapter Six: Saturday

Kitten Countdown: 1

Ella dragged Yasmin to the market,
early.

"Come on! Ooh, I do love going to
the market with my nan. Nan got a
pair of earrings really cheap last week.
Sort of lilac, all sparkly. I mean to have
my ears pierced soon as I can save up
the money. Oops! Hurry, we'll miss the
best stuff!"

They ran along the street, cut
through an alley and almost fell over

Mike and his big brother. They were
bent over a fierce-looking motorbike,
so absorbed that they didn't see the
girls. Yasmin was surprised. Mike looked
really happy!

"Hi, Jack!" called Ella. "Hi, Mike!"

Yasmin smiled at them cautiously.

"Oh, Ella. Hallo. Hi, Yas." Mike
turned back at once to the bike. His
brother waved a greasy hand.

"They'll be going to the rally," said
Ella. "Look! There's Nan!" They ran to
meet her.

The market was great fun. Yasmin
and Ella giggled happily as Nan beat
down a man selling scarves.

"Hand-knitted? Pull the other one,
young man! Machine-knit if ever I saw
it. And don't tell me that's pure wool!"
The man had cut the price in half
before she was done.

Yasmin bought a length of golden

ribbon to tie up her plaits. Ella bought
a tiny purse. "Not got much money,
don't need a big 'un," she explained
cheerfully.

Yasmin went home, almost happy.
But as soon as she got in, she began to
worry over the kitten again. No one
had phoned. None of her friends had
called. She held Thingamubob against
her cheek and let the kitten chew her
hair. She felt cold. She didn't know
where to turn next. Maybe Mum would
let her keep just the one kitten. After all,
Thingamubob was so very small . . .

She went through her chores in a
daze, trying to think of somebody she
could ask to take a kitten.

She went round to the paper shop
just before closing time, to ask if anyone
else had even looked at her card. But
no one had. Yasmin started for home.

She was trying so hard not to cry

that she never noticed the brick in her path. Her foot caught on it and she smacked down on the kerb. The hand she flung out to break her fall twisted under her.

Yasmin sat up slowly, curled around her hand. She couldn't seem to breathe properly. She made little mewing sounds of pain as she tried to straighten her fingers. Her feet were somewhere beside her but they didn't belong to her for the moment.

Presently she got her feet under her and rocked herself forward. She got half way up and had to sit down again. The pain in her hand made her dizzy. It felt hot, burning. She could hardly breathe for it.

"I've broken it," she explained to herself. "That's why it hurts so much."

What did you do with a broken hand? You ought to wind bandages around it and put it in a sling. "But I haven't any bandages. Nor a sling." A big hanky would do, or a scarf. She had no hanky and no scarf.

Then she heard the footsteps. Someone was coming! Yasmin looked round hopefully. Oh, if it were only a policewoman or one of her friends who would go for help . . . !

It was Mike. Mike, scowling and dragging his feet. Mike, in the worst rage she'd ever seen him in. She let out her breath with a gasp. No use asking Mike for help.

He stopped. He'd heard her. "Yas? What're you doing there?"

Yasmin kept her voice steady. "I fell and hurt myself. I'll be OK in a minute."

She heard her voice shake on the last word and a sob tried to force its way out of her chest. She swallowed it angrily. Mike came across the road and peered at her in the dim light.

"You really are hurt!" He sounded so surprised that Yasmin almost giggled. "Here, I'll help you." He reached out to take her hand. Yasmin drew back. Mike snatched his hand away at once.

He must think she didn't want his help!

"It's my hand. My right hand," she told him in a hurry. He stopped and bent down to her.

"Oh. I see. Well, take my hand and I'll help you up." He let her do the reaching. When she had firm hold of his arm, he gently pulled her up.

"There's a phone box in the next street. I could call an ambulance," he suggested. "You look awful!"

"Oh, thanks!" Yasmin giggled weakly. "But I'd rather go home. Mum will be worried."

"Right. Where do you live?"

They walked slowly. Yasmin felt shaky and weepy. Mike was quiet. After a bit, he asked where she'd been.

Yasmin explained about the kittens. It was just like Mike never to have noticed everyone else trying to find them homes!

"So today's the last day," he said.

Yasmin sighed. "Yes. There's only Thingamubob left." She stopped as Mike laughed. She'd never heard him laugh before.

"Thingamubob! Where'd you ever get a name like that?" he asked.

"She's the smallest, the last of the litter. It was Ella named her Thingamubob. She said she ought to have a long name to make up for being the littlest."

"Sounds like Ella. Sort of thing she would say." Mike's voice was flat. He had lost interest. He was gloomy again.

Yasmin told herself she wasn't being nosy. "Is . . . is something the matter? I mean, can you tell me what's wrong?"

Mike was holding her elbow as she stepped up a kerb. He let go and turned away from her. "Nothing's wrong. It's only . . ."

Yasmin shut her teeth against the jolt as she stumbled. Mike was holding her again at once. "Sit down." They'd reached the wooden bench by the recreation ground.

He sat beside her while she caught her breath. "See, it's my brother Jack. He was taking me to the rally on his bike." He stopped and stared at his feet.

"Yes, I saw you with him, this morning. Didn't you go in the end?"

"In the end! Oh, yes, he took me there. He took me all right."

Yasmin listened and said nothing.

"But his girlfriend turned up. Sylvie. At the rally. So he has to take her home, on his bike, don't he. So I don't matter no more. I can get the bus back, can't I, and be so late I miss my supper and it don't matter to Jack. *She's* the only thing matters! I don't matter no more. Not to him and not to Dad . . ."

Yasmin was careful not to look at him. He'd hate her to see him crying.

"But if you hadn't been late, I'd still be sitting by the side of the road, holding my arm," she whispered. "And crying because I couldn't stand up."

Mike looked at her. She thought he smiled. "Come on, then. Let's get you home," he said.

Mike's Diary

Sat.
Went biking with my brother Jack. He had his girlfriend meet him. So I had to go home by bus. Got mad.
Met Yas. She was

hurt. Helped her home.
Her mum took her to
hospital. She showed me
her kitten first. Silly
little scrap. It
purred at me.
Dad was
out when I
got home.
Wish I
could have
a cat.
Dad's dog
kills cats. I
hate that dog.
Dad don't care . . .
That Sylvie was there
when I got home. She
got all gooey when I
said why I was late.
She asked Jack could
they take me to the

chippie for some
supper. It was good.
She said she'd ask her
mum to take the last
kitten. She said anyway
Yas needn't fret, the
Cats Protection people
won't put down healthy
cats, not ever. I'll tell
Yas tomorrow, so she
don't get silly.

I reckon Sylvie's OK.
Maybe Jack's not so
bad.

Chapter Seven: Sunday

Kitten Countdown: 1

Ella's Diary
Sunday
Granma and Granpa took me out in
the car, like they do every Sunday.
(They're Mum's mum and dad.) We
went to the woods and Rick, that's
their dog, rolled in something
horrible (fox mess, Granpa says)
and Granma said he'd have to run
behind the car. But she didn't mean
it. We wiped him with grass and

Granpa had a bottle of fizzy water and poured it over and we wiped some more but he still ponged. I said to put him in the boot and we did. He howled all the way home. Mum made me have a bath. She

said I ponged too. Granpa and Granma went straight home to bath Rick. Mum had got a special tea for them but they couldn't stay.

Later
I just went round to see if Yas has
found a home for the last kitten
and she's been to hospital!
Yesterday! Well, last night. Mike
helped her home!!! She never told
me. Course, I was out ever so
early this morning. Her mum says
she's OK to go to school tomorrow.
But, would you believe, Mike came
round and said he'd maybe got a
home for Thingamubob!! His brother's
girlfriend's mum!

Mike's Diary
Sun.
Nothing much happened.
Granpa come to tea.
Asked if he knowed
anyone wants a kitten.
He don't. But Jack
says if Sylvie says she'll

do a thing, she does it.

Went round to Yas.
Her mum said thank you
again. That's 4 times. I
told them Sylvie reck-
ons her mum will take
the kitten. It's so
small. It purred for
me again. Yas will keep
it till tomorrow. Told
her what Sylvie said -
that it will be all right
even if it goes to the
Cat Protection. So she
starts snivelling!

This is the last diary
I'm ever writing.

Tonight Jack told Dad
all about Yas hurting
herself and all that.
Dad said I done well!

He's got good news too,
he says. He's got a new
job. No more night
shifts. We can all go to
the next rally, he says,
me and him and Jack
and Sylvie.

I reckon that'll be
OK.

Chapter Eight: Monday

Kitten Countdown: 1

Yasmin wasn't surprised that so many people wanted to know about her hand. The bandages made it stiff and the sling made everyone notice it.

Ella was eagerly telling people all about it. Yasmin was almost pleased for her to take over. A tiny bit of her still wanted to tell her own story, thank you, Ella! But she smiled and said nothing.

"So her mum called an ambulance

and they took them to the accident place at the hospital and they x-rayed Yasmin's hand — how many times, Yas?"

"Three times. I had to turn it over for them to take different views," explained Yasmin.

"Yes, three times and she's chipped the bone on her little finger and one of the teeny bones in her hand was pushed out of place — did you know there's ever so many little bones in your hand and wrist? — so they put it back and bandaged it all and she's not to use her hand for a bit, so's the chip settles down."

"It's a very small chip," Yasmin told the crowd around her. "So small it may be not worth cutting my finger open to take it out."

"Ooh, yuk!" said Katie. "Cutting it open! Double yuk!"

"Does it hurt?" asked Nick.

"A bit. If I knock it. It's bruised as well, you see."

"Hey, you can't write, can you? So you didn't finish your diary!"

Yasmin smiled. "Oh, but I did. Sort of. I had some help with yesterday's diary."

There was a scuffle across the

playground. Everyone went to see.

"Hey, listen to this!" shouted Alice. "Listen what Scotty wrote in his diary!"

Scott tried to grab the notebook. But Alice was taller than Scott. She was the tallest in the class. She held it out of his reach and read aloud: " *'Sunday: Put on Spiderman costume and swung up to rooftop to watch for criminals. Seeing a man come out of a roof, I swooped down and questioned him. He said he was a roofer. On a Sunday? I asked. I went into the house and found a lady all tied up and her jewel case empty.'* "

Alice stopped to let the sniggers die away. "It gets better!" She cleared her throat. "Hhrmm. *'I untied her and arrested the burglar, dropping him on the police station roof. The lady tried to kiss . . .'* "

Alice stopped. She was giggling too hard to go on.

Everybody was laughing. Scott was bright red. He howled with rage, snatched his notebook and turned to run for the toilets.

Yasmin stopped laughing. She was sure Scott was crying. I can't let them laugh at him, she thought. If it was me, I'd hate it. She felt brave, quite suddenly. Like a different person!

"It was a joke!" she said loudly. "A joke for Mr Williams. And you spoiled it, Alice."

Yasmin saw that Scott had stopped. He'd heard. Good!

Alice stopped sniggering. "So what?"

"I vote we all keep quiet about Scott's joke," Yasmin said. "I want to see Mr Williams' face when he reads it!" It was hard to keep her voice loud and steady. She would not let it shake!

Ella was staring at her, surprised. Yasmin nudged her, gently. Ella jumped. "Oh, yeah! Great idea, Yas! Let's give old Williams a surprise."

Scott came slowly back.
Katie grinned at him.
"That's a great idea,
Scotty. I really like it.
Wish I'd thought of it."

"Yeah, me too," said
Connor. "Hey, I could've
been a tight-rope walker!"

"I'd've been a ballerina!"
said Fen.

"A football star!"
shouted Patrick.

"A tennis
champion,"
said Alice.

Scott began
to smile. He
smoothed the
cover of his diary.
Nick joined him.
"I made out I was a policeman," he
said proudly. "*And* an SAS man!"

As they lined up to go in, Scott moved next to Yasmin.

"You found a home for all them kittens?" he asked, softly.

Yasmin shook her head. "One left."

"You still got it?"

She nodded. "Just till tonight." Her breath almost stopped. Hope hurt. Was he . . . had he found . . . ?

"Well, look, I'm sorry I said that about them killing the kittens. It's not true! I'm really sorry, Yas! You wasn't too upset?"

Yasmin made herself smile at him. "Thank you, Scott. It's all right now." She was so glad Sylvie had told Mike about it. And how lucky that Mike had come and told her last night! Or she might have cried in front of everyone.

Where *was* Mike? Late again? No, there he was, running across the play-ground, straight to her.

"It's all OK!" he gasped. "Sylvie rang up and she says her mum does want Thingamubob. She'll come round tonight for her!"

Yasmin felt a huge grin spreading over her face. "Thank you! Oh, thank you, Mike!" she said. "You are super!"

Yasmin's Diary
Sunday
This is Mike. I'm writing this for Yas. She's hurt her hand and can't write. She wants me to draw the last Kitten, so here it is.
This is Thingamubob.

Yas says it's better than her drawing. She's daft.

She wants to say she won't tear up her diary after all, mr williams, because it tells how she got homes for her Kittens and (she says I got to put this down) because she thinks I'm a good friend. All I done was take her home when she got hurt but Yas says she wants to Keep it in her diary. I reckon Yas is a good friend to have. She says I didn't ought to put that in but I've wrote it in ink so she can't rub it out. So there!

Kitten Countdown: None!

A WITCH IN THE CLASSROOM!
Ghillian Potts

"You're a frog, Ryan James, you're a frog.
Slimy and jumpy, bug-eyed and lumpy . . ."

Abigail is thrilled when she discovers that
she's a witch – at last she can get her own
back on her bullying classmate, Ryan.
With help from her pet rat, Gnasher, Abigail
turns Ryan into a frog, but that's when disaster
strikes – she can't change him back! And
suddenly Abigail discovers that she's not
the ONLY witch in the classroom . . .

This hilarious story will cast
a spell over all readers.

Young Corgi
0 552 54685 2

SINK OR SWIM
Ghillian Potts

"No, don't dive! Stop!"

William goes to the swimming baths every
week with the rest of his class, but he always
stays close to the side, scared of the water.
Then Big Mark dives in right on top of
him and pushes him underwater!

Nobody believes it was an accident.
Big Mark is always pushing people around.
He should be stopped. That's when William
comes up with a clever plan – a plan
that has surprising results.

Young Corgi
0 552 52753 X

PATRICK THE PARTY-HATER
Emily Smith

Balloons? Sausages on sticks?
An entertainer? Oh NO!
It must be a party...

Patrick loves making models and
creating his own inventions. He does
not love Musical Bumps, big crowds
and having to be jolly. But his mum is
convinced that going to parties is good
for him. She even wants him to have
one of his own. Surely there must
be a better idea?

A very special story from
a prize-winning author.

Young Corgi
0 552 55173 2